KU-483-531

Say Please, Little Bear

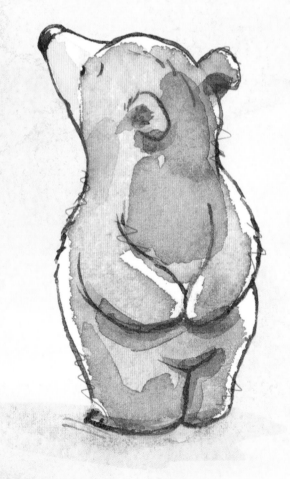

This edition published by Parragon in 2014
Parragon
Chartist House
15–17 Trim Street
Bath BA1 1HA, UK
www.parragon.com

Copyright © Parragon Books Ltd 2011-2014

All rights reserved. No part of this publication may be reproduced,
stored in a retrieval system or transmitted, in any form or by any means,
electronic, mechanical, photocopying, recording or otherwise, without
the prior permission of the copyright holder.

ISBN 978-1-4454-5560-0

Printed in China

Say Please, Little Bear

Story by Peter Bently

Illustrations by Robert McPhillips

Bath · New York · Cologne · Melbourne · Delhi
Hong Kong · Shenzhen · Singapore · Amsterdam

Daddy Bear and Little Bear were on their
way to playgroup.
But Little Bear kept wandering off.

"Keep hold of my hand, Little Bear!" said Daddy Bear.

"Go gently, Little Bear!"
said Daddy Bear at playgroup.

But Little Bear didn't listen.

"Little Bear, it isn't nice to snatch!"

"It's better when
we share, Little Bear,"
said Daddy Bear.

Later, Daddy Bear took Little Bear to
Little Bunny's birthday party.
They went shopping on the way.
"Please hold my hand, Little Bear!"
said Daddy Bear wearily.

Then something in the shop window
gave Daddy Bear an idea.
"Look, Little Bear," he said.
"Mouse wants to speak to us!"

TOY SHOP

"Mouse wants to come to the party too, Little Bear," said Daddy Bear. "But he hates to be late!"

They reached Little Bunny's party on time.
Mouse whispered in Daddy Bear's ear.

"Mouse says, excuse me, please,"
said Daddy Bear.

Little Bear ran to play on the train.
Mouse whispered in Daddy Bear's ear again.
"Mouse says,
can she have
a ride on the
train, please?"

Little Bear snatched the popcorn from his friends.
Mouse whispered in Daddy Bear's ear once again.
"Mouse says, would *you* like some popcorn,
Bunny and Mole?"

When it was
time to go,
Little Bear
stood silently
on the doorstep.
"Mouse says,
thank you for
having me,"
said Daddy Bear.

Little Bear looked at Mouse. Then he looked at Daddy Bear. Then he looked at Little Bunny's mummy and said, "And thank you for having me."

"Oh, thank you for coming, Little Bear,"
smiled Little Bunny's mummy.

"You and Mouse can
come and play any time."

"Mouse likes the way
you said thank you,"
said Daddy Bear.

"And so do I."

The story ends.

The sharing begins.